A Is for

EL!ZABETH

written by
Rachel Vail

illustrated by
Paige Keiser

Feiwel and Friends
New York

A FEIWEL AND FRIENDS BOOK
An imprint of Macmillan Publishing Group, LLC
175 Fifth Avenue, New York, NY 10010

Our books may be purchased in bulk for promotional,
educational, or business use. Please contact your local
bookseller or the Macmillan Corporate and Premium
Sales Department at (800) 221-7945 ext. 5442 or by email
at MacmillanSpecialMarkets@macmillan.com.

Library of Congress Cataloging-in-Publication Data
Names: Vail, Rachel, author. | Keiser, Paige, illustrator.
Title: A is for Elizabeth / by Rachel Vail ;
illustrated by Paige Keiser.
Description: First edition. | New York : Feiwel and Friends,
[2019] | Summary: Elizabeth, the second-grade sister of Justin Case,
is excited about her first homework assignment but it leads her
to start a protest of alphabetical order.
Identifiers: LCCN 2018039304| ISBN 9781250162120 (hardcover) |
ISBN 9781250162137 (ebook)
Subjects: | CYAC: Schools—Fiction. | Homework—Fiction. |
Fairness—Fiction. | Family life—Fiction.
Classification: LCC PZ7.V1916 Aag 2019 | DDC [E]—dc23
LC record available at https://lccn.loc.gov/2018039304

Book design by Liz Dresner
Feiwel and Friends logo designed by Filomena Tuosto

First edition, 2019
1 3 5 7 9 10 8 6 4 2
mackids.com

Chapter
1

Good news!

Ms. Patel told us today we have homework.

We are in second grade now.

So we get homework!

This is the day I've been waiting for!

The homework is: Make name posters.

Posters of our names!

I raised my hand.

"Elizabeth?" Ms. Patel said, smiling at me.

"Can we make anybody's name we want?" I asked. "In the whole 2B class?"

"No," said Ms. Patel. "You each make your own name."

That news was the opposite of good.

Chapter 2

"Some people have much longer names than other people," I explained to Ms. Patel.

"True," Ms. Patel said.

"Hey! That means some people will have to do more work," Bucky said.

Bucky's name is Bucky.

It has only five letters in it.

My name is Elizabeth.

It has a bajillion letters.

Bucky is my best friend.

"Be creative!" Ms. Patel said. "Have fun making your names!"

"That is not fair," I said.

"Not everything is fair," said Anna, without even raising her hand.

Anna is not my best friend.

Chapter 3

"And Friday, when you bring in your posters, we will hang them all up!" Ms. Patel said.

We all cheered. Class 2B will look so much better covered in posters!

"We will hang them around Class 2B in alphabetical order," Ms. Patel said.

Only some of us cheered at that news.

"Who can remind Class 2B what alphabetical order is?" Ms. Patel asked us. "Hands, please."

Anna's hand was the first one up.

Anna LOVES being first.

"In the order of the alphabet!" Anna yelled.

Ms. Patel hadn't even finished saying the whole name of Anna.

She was still on the *An*.

"Like, first *A* . . ." Anna said.

And she smiled that T. rex smile of hers.

"That's right," Ms. Patel said. "So we—"

"Then *B*," said Anna.

"Yes," said Ms. Patel. "So, we will hang—"

"Then C," Anna said.

"Thank you, Anna," said Ms. Patel.

"You're welcome," Anna said.

Chapter 4

After that, it was time for recess.

Anna was first in line. Of course.

Because of alphabetical order.

When we got to the swings, I
explained to her quietly, "Nobody
likes a show-off, Anna Banana."

Anna shrugged and said, "Sticks and stones may break my bones, but names will never hurt me."

Chapter
5

I don't know why sticks and stones
may break Anna's bones.

Maybe Anna is allergic to sticks
and stones.

Bucky is
allergic to
peanuts.

Chapter
6

Anna always gets to be first.

Her name poster will be first.

Also, Anna always gets to sit next
to my best friend, Bucky.

All because of the alphabet.

And its order.

And that *A* up at the front of her name.

A is for *Anna*.

A is also for *Annoying*.

Chapter 7

The *E* up at the front of my name, *Elizabeth*, is my problem.

It is the reason I am always stuck between Dan and Fiona.

Dan smells like sneakers and Fiona hardly talks at all.

Recess was done.

I had to line up to go back into
school between Smelly and Silent.

Chapter 8

Today in school, I was still writing my name when everybody else had already finished writing.

Today is Wednesday.

Wednesday is the worst day to write. It has so many extra letters.

Like my name.

My extra letters leaked down the side of my paper.

Now it is Wednesday night.

I have not started my name poster.

Why oh why did those parents name me such a long thing as *Elizabeth*?

Chapter 9

Hooray for today because it is
Thursday, and I finally got a great
idea for my poster!

There is only one problem with it.

THINGS I AM NOT ALLOWED TO BRING INTO THE HOUSE

1. Sticks
2. Rocks
3. A bad attitude

THINGS I BROUGHT INTO THE HOUSE TODAY

1. Sticks
2. Rocks
3. A bad attitude

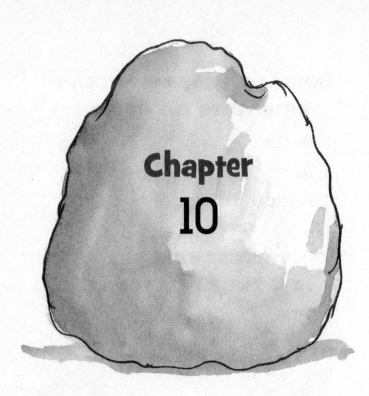

Chapter 10

Well.

I had good reasons.

ALPHABETICAL ORDER is the good reason I brought a bad attitude into our house all week.

I did not have a good reason for bringing in the rocks.

Chapter
11

Hang on. I had TWO reasons to bring in rocks.

One of the reasons is a good reason!

The good reason is: decoration.

Decoration is good.

Like on a birthday cake.

Or, if you have time and bubbles,
on your head in the bath.

Chapter
12

The other reason for bringing rocks
into the house is a not good reason.

It is the kind of reason that is the
opposite of good.

It is because *rocks* means the same
thing as *stones*.

And because of the thing that Anna
said about her bones.

Chapter
13

One of the reasons I brought the sticks into the house is a GOOD reason.

It is:

I will make the letters on my name poster out of sticks.

I will glue the letters made of sticks onto poster board.

That is a creative and fun idea!

I will have the best name poster in

Class 2B!

Chapter
14

I ran downstairs to tell my parents the exciting news about my project.

"I have homework to do tonight!" I told them. "And I collected the supplies all by myself!"

"What supplies?" asked Mom.

I did not want to get in trouble about the rocks or the sticks.

"Never mind about that," I told her. "All I need now is poster board!"

"Poster board?" asked Dad.

"Yes," I said. "For my homework."

"Elizabeth," said Mom. "It's after dinnertime!"

"The store closes at six p.m., Elizabeth!" said Dad.

"Daddy will have to drive all over Kingdom Come to find poster board at this time of night!" Mom yelled.

"Me?" Dad asked her.

"Woof woof woof!" added our dog, Qwerty.

"What is *Kingdom Come*?" I
asked. "Is that a real place? Are
there dragons in Kingdom Come? Do
dragons like poster board?"

Chapter
15

There is a rule in our family that I forgot all about.

It is:

No saying the words Poster Board after 6:00 p.m.

Chapter
16

"You said it, too," I told Mom.

"Said what?" she asked me.

"The words that rhyme with *toaster sword* . . ."

"Toaster sword?" she asked.

"Yes," I said.

I whispered the words *poster board*.

"You said those words at least five seconds later in the night than I did, Mom."

Mom shook her head.

Dad shook his head.

They both did loud breathing.

That is what they do when I make a good point and win the argument.

Even if there is no trophy involved,
I love winning.

I am not a sore winner, no matter
what Anna the Annoying says.

I am the opposite of sore.

I am a feel-great winner.

Chapter
17

Dad plucked his keys off the hook
and asked, "Do we need anything else
while I'm out?"

My big brother, Justin, didn't need
anything.

Of course.

"No, thanks," he said.

Mom rubbed his curly hair like he
was her good-luck charm.

"Well," I said. "Actually, some
strong glue would probably be a good
idea."

"Strong glue?" Mom asked.

"To glue my sticks onto the—you know. Thing that rhymes with *boaster floored*." I whispered the last part.

Chapter 18

"Sticks?" Mom asked.

Chapter
19

WHAT I TOLD MOM ABOUT WHY I AM MAKING MY NAME OUT OF STICKS:

"Other kids are doing glitter."

Last time I used glitter, Mom said, "Glitter is a nightmare."

She threw all the glitter in the

garbage, even the glitter that didn't have glue or our dog in it.

WHAT MOM SAID ABOUT STICKS INSTEAD OF GLITTER: "Sticks are a fine idea."

WHAT I DIDN'T TELL MOM ABOUT WHY I AM MAKING MY NAME OUT OF STICKS: The truth.

Chapter
20

I had an idea!
I ran
downstairs.
"Maybe you
could call Daddy," I
said.

"Why?" Mom asked.

"To ask if he can get the biggest piece of *you know what* that they have in the kingdom."

"What kingdom?" Mom asked.

"Kingdom Come," I said.

"That's an expression," Mom said.

"Well, whichever kingdom where he is buying the . . . thing that rhymes with *floaster snored!*"

"There's no kingdom," Mom said.

"So why did you say Daddy was going there?"

"Elizabeth," Mom said. "When did Ms. Patel tell you about this project?"

"Tuesday," I told her.

"Elizabeth!" said Mom. "Today is Thursday!"

"I know! I meant to ask every day, but then, every day? I forgot," I explained.

"Elizabeth," she said again.

"I'm still new at homework," I said.

"True," Mom said, and she rubbed my hair.

Sometimes I am her good-luck charm.

Chapter
21

Mom called Dad.

I danced around,
very happy again
about my
project.

The reason
I needed the

most gigantic poster board of all of Class 2B is:

The name *Elizabeth* has a bajillion letters in it!

So maybe I will have the biggest poster in the whole Class 2B!

The name *Anna* has only two letters to start it, and then those same two letters, backing up. You could do a whole project of that little name on a Post-it Note.

Chapter 22

I twirled around my room waiting
for Dad to get home from Not A
Kingdom.

I tried to make some room on my
desk for doing homework.

My brother, Justin, is not the only
one with homework now.

I have a new desk in my room.

I have my own set of markers.

I have a great idea.

Soon I will be at the front of
everything.

Chapter 23

There was not enough room on my desk.

I spread the sticks and stones out on my rug.

I looked at them.

My dog, Qwerty, looked, too.

I could tell he thought my idea was the opposite of good.

He kept trying to take those sticks away.

Qwerty is a dog.

He has never had homework.

But I was a little bit worrying that maybe he was right, anyway.

Because I kept imagining a very scary thing:

Me in Class 2B tomorrow, holding my poster board with my name made out of sticks and stones.

And then all of Anna's bones, breaking.

Maybe I should borrow Justin's markers instead.

I could promise to not press so hard
I smoosh their heads in.

I'll ask him.

Anna is a show-off, but I don't
really want all her bones to break.

Chapter
24

Maybe only one small bone.

Maybe just a sprain.

Anna could go to the nurse's office and sit on the crinkle-paper bench.

She could relax for a while with her sprained bone.

Instead of smiling all the time right in everybody's face.

Chapter 25

Justin said no to borrowing his markers.

He said I always smoosh their heads in.

He asked, "Why don't you use your own markers?"

I said, "Because their heads are all smooshed in."

chapter 26

I used the drippy glue Dad bought,
and all my rocks and sticks.

I showed Justin how cool it looked
when I finished.

"You used so much glue," he said.

"I needed it," I said.

"Your sticks are like kayaks in glue ponds," he said.

"They're not kayaks," I said. "They are letters."

"What are you making?" he asked.

"My name," I explained.

"I thought your name was Elizabeth," he said.

Chapter
27

"Sometimes the name *Elizabeth* starts
with the letter *A*," I explained to
Justin.

"No it doesn't," he said.

Justin is in fifth grade, so he thinks he knows everything.

"Sometimes it does," I said.

"Never," he said.

"Haven't you ever heard of *sound it out*?" I asked.

Justin looked confused. Ha! Even fifth graders don't know everything.

"*Annoying. Amazing,*" I said. "Sound it out. What letter makes the *uh* sound at the beginning?"

"An *A*," Justin said.

"AHA!" I said. "And my name starts with the same sound! *A*-lizabeth!"

"But your name starts with *E*," he said.

"Sometimes," I said.

"Always!"

"Also, sometimes my name has a bunch of *M*s in it. Like a whole little set of mountains."

*M*s take so many of the little sticks.

"No!" Justin said. "There are no *M*s in Elizabeth!"

"Sometimes there are rocks in my name, like this! They are sometimes the dot."

"The dot?" Justin asked. "What even is that?"

"It is called an ex-pla-nation point," I said as my ex-pla-nation.

"Ex-CLA-mation point!" Justin yelled. "It's an ex-CLA-mation point, not an ex-PLA-nation point!"

"Yeah, well, stop explaining, then!" I yelled at him.

He can be very frustrating.

"But, Elizabeth," he said. "Names don't have—"

"I have three of those points in my name," I exPLained.

"No, you don't," said Justin.

"See? I do!" I showed him. "But sometimes the rocks make the letter

O. Sometimes my name has seven *O*s in it."

"No, it doesn't!" Justin yelled louder. "It has zero *O*s! Your name is spelled *E-L-I-Z-A-B-E-T-H*!"

"Sometimes," I agreed.

"ALWAYS! ALWAYS!" Justin shouted. "THAT IS HOW SPELLING WORKS!"

"Maybe for *your* name," I said.

Chapter
28

The poster did not look the way I had planned.

Some of the sticks and stones had trouble staying where I put them.

Sometimes I have trouble staying put, too.

So I get it.

But still.

All Mom and Dad care about is bedtime, even when there is a poster crisis.

Chapter
29

I cuddled up cozy with Dolores, my stuffed dog-rabbit.

Her one eye and my two eyes all stayed open.

We were having trouble with settling down.

The gluey project on my rug was why.

Every time we closed our three eyes, it felt like all the letters got up off my poster and danced around my room together.

While they danced, the stick-letters and the stone-letters sang a song in their teasing sticks-and-stones voices.

The tune didn't matter, but the words kept repeating:

Alphabetical order! Alphabetical order!

Chapter
30

"I thought you were making your name," Mom said at breakfast.

"It is my name," I said.

"But isn't that an *A*?" Mom asked. "And some of those look like exclamation points."

"Don't even try," Justin told her.

"It's an abstract version," I said.

"Oh," Mom said.

"Cool," Dad said.

I felt as unsure as their faces looked.

I said, "We are supposed to be creative in Class 2B."

And I looked as brave as I ever could.

Chapter 31

It was a rough walk to the bus stop.

Not all of my rocks made it.

Luckily, my name is not as strict about spelling as some people's names.

At least the *A* at the start of my name was sticking.

And the other *A* next to that first *A*, too.

I needed both those *A*s at the beginning.

When two names start with the same first letter, you look at the next letter.

And think about the alphabet.

That is the rule of alphabetical order.

Anna has an *N* next to her first *A*.

My name when you spell it *AAbAmmm!moxooo!Eoo'oAth!* comes way before *Anna*.

Because: alphabetical order.

It was okay about the falling-off rocks.

I didn't need all the *O*s.

Some of them were for decoration.

It's my name.

I should know how to spell it.

"Yes, you should," Justin said.

Chapter 32

My name poster and I needed a bus
seat all to ourselves.

My best friend Bucky's poster
was rolled up with a red rubber band
around it.

His was on the skinnier kind of
poster board called oaktag.

He is gentler with markers than I am.

And his mom allows the awesome oily crayon things that ruined our couch.

We don't have those anymore in our family.

Bucky sat in a bus seat with Mallory instead of with me today.

Mallory was in the other first grade class, so we hardly know her.

Her headband had cat ears on it.

Her poster was rolled up too.

I was starting to feel like maybe I didn't do it right.

The poster.

Anything.

Chapter 33

I didn't know there was going to be
Tell About Your Poster.

Each kid has to stand up and tell
something.

You can tell a fact about your name.

You can tell about the artwork you
did.

I am not afraid to stand up in front of the class and say things.

I used to be afraid when I was little, but I'm not anymore.

Shy is not the reason maybe I might hide under my desk.

It's that my name looked like it was melting off my poster.

And Anna's name looked very
pretty on her poster.

Also:

I didn't want to tell the reason I
used sticks and stones.

Chapter
34

Luckily, I had some time while

Anna

Bucky

Cade H.

Cade Z.

Cali

Cullen

And then Smelly Dan had their turns telling about their names and posters.

Chapter
35

I didn't listen nicely while the other kids said things.

I didn't come up with a good thing to tell.

Instead I spent my time thinking the word *UH-OH*.

And trying not to hide under my desk.

Maybe I could tell about the points!

I couldn't remember if it's actually exPLanation points or exCLamation points.

Nobody else in 2B had any.

So maybe they really aren't supposed to be in the middle of our names.

Maybe my brother was right.

He had very strong opinions about the topic.

"*Elizabeth?*" said Ms. Patel.

Uh-oh.

Chapter
36

I walked slowly to the front of the room.

I carried my poster board,
decorated in sticks and stones and
dried lakes of glue.

A few rocks fell off along the way.

I was not feeling proud of how that
huge poster looked.

Or of myself for making it.

Chapter 37

I tried to make my mouth say
abstract.

Or *creative.*

Or *A terrible accident on the bus
ride to school.*

No luck.

My mouth stayed clamped shut.

My fingers were making dimples in the poster board.

"Elizabeth?" Ms. Patel said quietly. "Would you like to tell us about your poster?"

A rule in our family is **Tell the truth.**

So I said, "No."

Chapter
38

Ms. Patel smiled kindly at me.

"Do you want to sit down for now?"
Ms. Patel asked.

"No," I answered.

"You can have another chance
after the other students go," she said.
"Maybe you'll get inspired."

I tried to tell my feet to walk back
to my seat.

My feet said NO.

None of me was behaving.

"Elizabeth?" Ms. Patel asked. "Do
you want to take a seat?"

"No," I said.

"Would you like to tell us about your poster, then?" she asked.

"No," I said.

Some of the kids were giggling.

I don't know which kids because I was looking at my poster.

It was a mess.

"Elizabeth," Ms. Patel said.

"It's not fair," I said.

"What's not fair?" Ms. Patel asked.

"Alphabetical order," I said.

Now a lot of kids were giggling.

"Why does *A* always get to be first?" I asked.

"Yeah," said Bucky.

Bucky is always on my side, even when he sits next to somebody else on the bus.

That is why he's my best friend.

"How do you think that makes the letter *E* feel?" I asked the class. "Never getting to be first?"

"Or the letter *B*?" Bucky said.

"How about *Z*?" Zora added quietly.

"Yeah," I said. "Poor Z!"

"Yeah," Bucky said.

"How do you think Z feels?" I asked Ms. Patel. "Always being last?"

"Like the caboose," Zora said.

"What's *caboots*?" Smelly Dan asked.

"A kind of farm in Israel," Cullen said. "My aunt lived on one!"

"Wait," Bucky said. "Why does a Z feel like a farm in Israel?"

"She said *BOOTS*," Mallory said. "Z feels like *BOOTS*. Like, down in the mud."

"I don't think *E* and *B* and *Z* feel like anything," Takara said. "They're letters."

"Quiet, please," Ms. Patel said.

Chapter 40

Anna raised her hand. She waggled it around.

"Anna?" Ms. Patel asked. "Do you have a question?"

"No," Anna said. "I have a statement. Or a comment. I think it's a comment."

"Elizabeth is presenting her name poster," Ms. Patel said.

"Well, her poster has no name on it," Anna argued.

"Yes it does," I said. "It has the name *Elizabeth* on it."

Everybody looked at my poster.

Nobody said *Yes, there is her name, Elizabeth, of course!*

Not even Bucky.

Chapter
41

I took a big breath.

"It is unfair that Z never gets to be first, or E, for example," I said. "Other letters should have a turn being first in the alphabetical order."

"Like B!" Bucky yelled. "B always has to be second place. That's not fair!"

"Yeah," a lot of kids said, and told their letters, and how unfair alphabetical order is to them.

Not Fiona, of course. She never says anything.

But a lot of other kids were shouting their first letters.

"Especially Z," Zora yelled.

"See?" I said to Ms. Patel. "Alphabetical order is unfair. That's what I want to say about my name poster. I want to say: This is *not* a name poster. It is a protest sign."

I held my poster above my head.

My friends cheered.

Chapter
42

A protest was not my plan.

My plan was:

My Name Actually Starts with the Letter A! Twice! Surprise! So I Should Be First!

Also, *Sticks and stones may break Anna's bones.*

A rule in our family is: **Stand up for what you believe in.**

WHAT I BELIEVE IN

1. Fairness
2. Take turns
3. Sound it out
4. I want to be first

Mostly, I believe in numbers 1 and 4 from that list.

Ms. Patel is a very nice teacher. She has a quiet voice.

She has crinkles near her eyes and mooshy gooshy arms.

Saying *Alphabetical order is unfair* was standing up for what I believe in.

But saying it to a person like

Ms. Patel, who believes in alphabetical order, is hard.

It made my bones feel like they might all break.

And that's when I realized a terrible thing:

Maybe I am allergic to sticks and stones, too.

Chapter
43

Anna raised her hands again and waggled them around in the air so much.

She was bouncing in her seat saying, "Ooh! Ooh! Ooh! Ms. Patel!"

"Anna," said Ms. Patel.

"Alphabetical order is just the order of the alphabet," Anna said. "Right?"

"Right," said Ms. Patel. "Thank you, Anna."

"You're welcome," Anna said. "Right, Elizabeth? It's just the order of the alphabet?"

"Yes," I said. "Sure."

I was tired, honestly. Protesting is hard work.

"So there is nothing to protest," Anna said. "You can't protest a fact."

"Didn't you ever hear of *take turns*?" I asked her.

"Yeah," Bucky said. "Take turns is a fact, too."

"You might like alphabetical order, Anna," I said. "But it is not fair that *A* always gets to be the first letter!"

"You might *not* like alphabetical order, Elizabeth," Anna said right back. "But not liking a thing doesn't make it unfair."

Chapter 44

Well, true.

But Anna being right did not stop me from wanting to smash my poster board over her head.

Still, I didn't.

Because: *Sticks and stones may break her bones.*

And: *My name (poster) might really hurt her.*

Another rule in our family is: **No hitting anybody over the head with your stuff, Elizabeth.**

So I just stood there in the front of my class, waiting for Ms. Patel to sort this problem out.

Chapter
45

A strange thing was happening in the seat next to my empty seat.

Silent Fiona was raising her hand. Fiona never raises her hand.

She raised that hand slowly.

She pushed it up into the classroom air, where it had never been raised before.

Fiona's face looked sad about what her hand was doing.

"Fiona?" Ms. Patel asked. "Did you want to say something?"

Fiona didn't answer that question.

Fiona never talks, but she always tries to get the right answer.

I was her math buddy one time in first grade, so I know.

Even when you're Fiona's buddy, you hardly hear her voice.

Fiona closed her eyes and opened her mouth.

Chapter
46

"Maybe it doesn't have to be a
conflict," Fiona said.

Her voice was quiet.

But it wasn't shaky.

"What did she say?" Smelly Dan
asked.

"Shhh," Bucky told him.

"What do you mean, Fiona?" Ms. Patel asked.

I rested my big poster on the toe of my sneaker because it was getting heavy.

"I don't think we can just say good-bye to alphabetical order," Fiona said.

"Of course not!" Anna said. "It's just a thing. It just *is*."

"All the letters would be in a jumble if we got rid of alphabetical order," Fiona said, a little louder. "The dictionary would be a mess."

"But what about *fairness*?" I said.

"Don't we care about *fairness* and *take turns* in this class?"

"Yeah," Bucky said.

"Fairness!" Zora said.

That made me look down at my poster on my shoe.

It was garbage.

If my original plan had worked, Zora would still be last, like a farm in Israel or muddy boots.

Zora is a smarty-pants, but she is also fun.

She should get a turn being first sometimes, probably.

"But maybe," Fiona said. "Maybe alphabetical order isn't the *only* order."

"We could do height order!" said Babyish Cali, who is shortest in 2B.

"Yeah!" said Mallory, who is tallest.

"Or whose birthday is the highest number," said Bucky.

His birthday is December 31.

"Or the lowest number!" said Smelly Dan.

I don't know when his birthday is, but I have a guess:

Beginning of an early month.

"Or who finishes the math sheet fastest," said Zora.

That is a thing she is *always* first at.

Chapter
47

Everybody had suggestions.

We all yelled them out until Ms. Patel raised *her* hand.

She is the teacher.

The teacher raising her hand?

We got quiet.

"These are terrific ideas," she said. "Every project needs teamwork to work."

She got out her fat marker and huge pad and wrote down all our ideas.

In just the order we thought of them.

Chapter
48

We hung up our name signs in an
order called random.

Mine was right in the middle of the back wall.

Ms. Patel said she loves the !s in my name.

I do, too.

We lined up to go out for recess in height order, shortest to tallest.

We lined up for the swings in age order, oldest to youngest.

We lined up to go back inside in curliest hair to straightest.

It was more of a clump than a line

because it's hard to agree whose hair is curliest.

Then we lined up to go to music in a different kind of alphabetical order.

Backward alphabetical order.

Zora was first.

Anna was last.

The music teacher is a bit of a yeller.

So I didn't mind being toward the caboose.

Chapter 49

Turns out a caboose is the last part of a train.

Zora told me during music class.

"I knew that," I said. "I just forgot."

"You thought she said *BOOTS*," Anna said.

"No, I did not!" I said. "That was Mallory who said that! I am the one who said it's unfair that . . ."

"You said a lot of things!" Anna yelled.

"So did you!" I yelled back. "And are you allergic to sticks?"

"No!" Anna yelled.

"Are you allergic to stones?"

"NO!" Anna yelled. "Nobody is allergic to sticks or stones! What are you even talking about?"

"Just making sure!" I yelled. "I didn't want your bones to break!"

"Well, thank you!" Anna yelled.

"QUIET!" Ms. Mooney yelled at both of us.

"You're welcome," I whispered to Anna.

When music was done, we lined up in order of quietest to noisiest.

Fiona got to be the line leader, even though she spoke up today.

She deserved the first spot.

She had been quiet for a long time, before this morning.

Also, she had a really good idea.

Everybody was liking Fiona so much today.

Including me.

She didn't say anything, leading us back from music.

But she sure looked proud.

Chapter
50

Anna and I were the noisy caboose together.

It wasn't bad.

Actually, it was the opposite of bad.

Acknowledgments

With thanks and love to:

Amy Berkower, who has long pushed for Elizabeth to have her say

Liz Szabla, who helped me find Elizabeth's punch and rhythm, and propel her to life

Jean Feiwel, feisty and strong like Elizabeth, and thus her guardian spirit

Paige Keiser, who finds (and shows) the soul and heart in each of these characters

The alphabet, for its unrelenting order

Zachary and Liam, first readers forever, whose questions and stories are my always inspiration

Mitch Elkind, who unfailingly believes that a tough, smart girl full of fight and feelings is the best

Mom and Dad, who taught me to share, speak up, and compromise, and also sometimes to not

Carin Berger, awesome at protest signs and glue but even better at friendship

Meg Cabot, hilarious and super-supportive fellow-traveler

Justin Case, worrier, warrior, fictional but so real to me, for introducing me to his awesome little sister

And all the kids and grown-ups who fight—kindly but persistently—to be heard, to defend their friends, and to do what's right

Thank you for reading this Feiwel and Friends book.

The Friends who made

A Is for

EL!ZABETH

possible are:

Jean Feiwel, Publisher

Liz Szabla, Associate Publisher

Rich Deas, Senior Creative Director

Holly West, Senior Editor

Anna Roberto, Senior Editor

Val Otarod, Associate Editor

Kat Brzozowski, Senior Editor

Alexei Esikoff, Senior Managing Editor

Kim Waymer, Senior Production Manager

Anna Poon, Assistant Editor

Emily Settle, Associate Editor

Starr Baer, Senior Production Editor

Liz Dresner, Associate Art Director

Follow us on Facebook or visit us online at mackids.com

Our books are friends for life.